P9-CPZ-807

The Princess and the Pea

A Viking Easy-to-Read Classic

retold by Harriet Ziefert
illustrated by Emily Bolam

VIKING

VIKING
Published by the Penguin Group
Penguin Books USA Inc., 375 Hudson Street, New York, New York 10014, U.S.A.
Penguin Books Ltd, 27 Wrights Lane, London W8 5TZ, England
Penguin Books Australia Ltd, Ringwood, Victoria, Australia
Penguin Books Canada Ltd, 10 Alcorn Avenue, Toronto, Ontario, Canada M4V 3B2
Penguin Books (N.Z.) Ltd, 182-190 Wairau Road, Auckland 10, New Zealand

Penguin Books Ltd, Registered Offices: Harmondsworth, Middlesex, England

First published in 1996 by Viking, a division of Penguin Books USA Inc.
Published simultaneously in Puffin Books

1   3   5   7   9   10   8   6   4   2

Text copyright © Harriet Ziefert, 1996
Illustrations copyright © Emily Bolam, 1996
All rights reserved

LIBRARY OF CONGRESS CATALOGING-IN-PUBLICATION DATA

Ziefert, Harriet.
The princess and the pea / retold by Harriet Ziefert ;
illustrated by Emily Bolam   p.   cm.—(Viking easy-to-read)
"A Viking easy-to-read classic."
Adaptation of : Prindsessen paa ærten / H.C. Andersen.
Summary: The queen has a plan to help the prince find a real princess to marry.
ISBN 0-670-86054-9
[1. Fairy tales.] I. Bolam, Emily, ill. II. Andersen, H.C. (Hans Christian), 1805–1875.
Prindsessen paa ærten. English. III. Title IV. Series.
PZ8.Z54Pr 1996 [E]—dc20 95-39341 CIP AC
Printed in U.S.A.
Set in Bookman

Viking® and Easy-to-Read® are registered trademarks of Penguin Books USA Inc.

Reading Level 1.8

The Princess and the Pea

There once was a prince,
who wanted to marry a princess.
But she had to be a *real* princess.

The prince looked and looked.
He met many princesses.

Many, many princesses!
Many, many, many princesses!

But the prince sent
all of them away.
He did not think they
were *real* princesses.

One day there was a big storm.
A princess knocked at the door.

"Come in," said the king.
"Come in," said the queen.

Oh, what a drippy princess!

Her hair was drippy!

Her dress was drippy!

Her shoes were drippy!

But still she said
she was a *real* princess.

The queen said, "I will see.
I will see if this is a *real* princess."
And she went off to make the bed.

First the queen
put a tiny pea
under the mattress.

Next, the queen put
1...2...3...4...5...
6...7...8...9...10...
mattresses on top of the pea.

Then she put
1... 2... 3... 4... 5...
6... 7... 8... 9... 10 more
mattresses on top of them.

On top of the twenty mattresses,
the queen put twenty down covers.

Then she called the princess.
"Your bed is ready!" she said.

The princess went to bed.

Oh, what a sleepy princess!

In the morning the queen asked,
"How did you sleep?"

And the king asked,
"How did you sleep?"

And the prince asked,
"How did you sleep?"

"I did not sleep,"
   said the princess.
"I did not sleep at all!
   I did not sleep because there
   was a big lump in my bed."

The queen smiled.
The king smiled.

"You must be a *real* princess!" they said.

"Only a *real* princess could feel a pea under twenty mattresses!"

The prince married the princess, because he knew she was a *real* princess!

And the pea?
They saved it for ever and ever.